THE
TIME MACHINE

Library of Congress Cataloging-in-Publication Data

James, Raymond.
　　The time machine / by H.G. Wells; retold by Raymond James;
illustrated by Jim Deal.
　　　　p.　　cm. (Troll illustrated classics)
　　Summary: A scientist invents a time machine and uses it to travel
hundreds of thousands of years into the future, where he discovers
the childlike Eloi and the hideous underground Morlocks.
　　ISBN 0-8167-2872-0 (lib. bdg.)　　　ISBN 0-8167-2873-9 (pbk.)
　　[1. Time travel—Fiction.　2. Science fiction.]　I. Deal, Jim,
1956-　　ill.　II. Wells, H.G. (Herbert George), 1866-1946.　Time
machine.　III. Title.
PZ7.J1543Ti　1993
[Fic]—dc20　　　　　　　　　　　　　　92-5804

THE TIME MACHINE

H.G. WELLS

Retold by
Raymond James

Illustrated by
Jim Deal

Troll Associates

Wind rippled through the parlor, yet the doors and windows were shut tight. A candle on top of the fireplace mantel suddenly blew out, yet no smoke or ash blew from the fireplace itself. And the flame in the table lamp flickered wildly as the tiny machine next to it started to turn around and around.

None of us could take our eyes off the machine before us. No bigger than a small clock, it was made of quartz, brass, ivory, and ebony. It was beautiful. Even now, three years later, I can still see in my mind how it glittered in the light.

Faster and faster went the machine until it became a blur. Soon, it looked like a ghost of itself—so faint and pale had

it become in the whirling. A second passed, then *poof*! The machine was gone. Vanished. Only the lamp still stood on the table.

I was thunderstruck by what I had just seen. I glanced at my fellow dinner guests: the psychologist, the doctor, the mayor, the very young man, and Filby. They were as shocked and silent as I was myself. Then the psychologist blinked hard and stooped down to look under the table. He passed his hand underneath it.

Our host laughed. "Well?"

The psychologist walked over to the fireplace mantel. He leaned against it, as if he needed something solid to hold on to.

"Look here," sputtered the doctor, visibly shaken. "Do you seriously believe that your little machine has traveled into time?"

"Certainly," said our host. There was not a trace of hesitation in his voice.

For the past hour or so, he had been trying to convince the six of us that movement was possible in more than just the three dimensions of length, width, and height. He felt absolutely sure that movement was possible in a *fourth* dimension—time.

The psychologist was among the first to doubt him. "Proof is in the seeing, not the talking," insisted the psychologist earlier in the evening. "After all, this is England in the middle of the 1890s, *not* the 890s. I'll believe it when I see it."

That's when our host brought out the tiny machine, a model he had been working on for two years. It was, he said, a time machine. There were two white levers on it. Pushing the first lever forward would make the machine glide into the future, he said. Pushing the second lever forward would slow the machine down or make it go backward in time.

The psychologist, at our host's urging, had set the machine into motion by pushing the first lever forward with his finger.

I was still thinking of the doctor's question—had the machine really disappeared into time—when our host spoke again. "I have a much bigger machine nearly finished in my laboratory, gentlemen," he said. "Would you like to see it?"

Without waiting for a reply, our host took the table lamp and started down a long corridor. We trailed after him. I was still numb from what I saw—or *thought* I saw. Somehow, I felt it was no fake. And yet . . .

"Gentlemen," said our host, opening the door to his laboratory, "behold my time machine!"

There, in the light cast from his lamp, we saw a full-scale version of the model that had vanished from the parlor table. This larger machine seemed almost complete. Only a few parts were missing, scattered on a workbench beside some drawings.

Our host held the lamp higher so that its light took in the entire machine before us. "In that," he said, gesturing toward the machine, "I intend to explore time."

I hurried as fast as I could to our host's home. I was late for dinner, scheduled for seven o'clock. A week had gone by since he had shown us his time travel "trick," as the doctor had called it. Already in the drawing room were other invited guests, including the doctor and the psychologist from before. Among four new guests was the editor of a popular daily newspaper.

"It's half-past seven now," said the doctor, holding a sheet of paper in one hand and his watch in the other. "I suppose we'd better have dinner."

"Where's— " I started to ask.

"Who knows?" the doctor said abruptly. "He says in this note to go ahead with dinner if he's not back. Says he'll explain when he gets here."

"What is this all about anyway?" the editor asked as we all headed for the dining room.

The psychologist tried to explain. He was in the middle of his remarks when the door from the corridor opened suddenly. Standing before us was our host.

"Good heavens, man, what's the matter?" cried the doctor at the sight of him.

Our host was in terrible shape. His coat was dusty and smeared with green along the sleeves. His hair was uncombed and wild, and he was ghastly pale. His chin had a half-healed cut on it. Clearly, he was exhausted.

He didn't say a word, but sat down at the table and quickly gulped a glass of water. Then he sat back and let out a long breath.

"That's good," he said, more to himself than us. Then he looked up at us standing around him. "I'm going to wash and dress, gentlemen. Then I'll come down and explain things . . . things you can't imagine."

He got up from the table and walked toward the staircase. It was then that I and the others saw his feet. He had nothing on them but a pair of tattered, blood-stained socks, and he walked with a limp.

The newspaper editor tried to make a joke to ease our shock. "Well, if he *has* traveled into the future, one can only wonder why there aren't any clothes brushes there. His coat is a mess."

Another new guest smiled. But the rest of us didn't. Even as we began to eat our dinner, I could see the worried looks on the faces of the doctor and the psychologist.

It wasn't long before our host returned, dressed in ordinary evening clothes. His face, though still haggard, was clean again.

"I say," the editor declared to our host, "these chaps here seem to think you may have been traveling into the middle of next week! Tell us about it, will you?"

Our host smiled, then sat down at the table. The editor may have thought of the whole thing as a joke or a stunt, but I sensed something very serious was at the heart of the matter.

"*Have* you been time traveling?" I asked pointblank.

"Yes," answered our host, rapidly finishing his food. "But it's too long a story to tell over greasy plates. I suggest we move to the parlor, gentlemen."

We all got up and walked into the parlor. There, our host continued.

"I will tell you the story of what happened to me," he said. "But you must not interrupt me. I want to tell it while it's still fresh in my mind. It may sound like a lie, but I assure you it isn't." He looked at us with a steely gaze. "No interruptions at all. Do you agree?"

"Agreed," said the editor. The rest of us nodded and said the same.

Slumping into a chair, our host began to speak. What follows is *his* story in *his* words, as clearly as I can remember them and write them down.

The Time Traveler Tells His Story

Since our last dinner together a week ago, I have worked night and day to complete my time machine. But it was not until this morning at ten o'clock that the machine was ready. I gave it a last tap, tried all the screws again, and put one more drop of oil on a quartz rod. Then I sat in the seat of the machine itself.

"I pressed the first lever forward and the second one right afterward. Immediately, my senses reeled. I felt as if I were falling. Then the feeling stopped. I looked around my laboratory. Everything was exactly the same as before. Nothing happened, I thought.

"But then I noticed the clock. When I had climbed into the machine, the time had read a minute past ten. Now, it was nearly half-past three!

"Taking a deep breath, I gripped the first lever again and pushed it forward. The hands of the laboratory clock whirred like the blades of a fan. Night came like the turning out of a lamp, and in another moment came tomorrow. Tomorrow night came, then day again, night again, day again, faster and faster still.

"Suddenly, the walls and the rest of the laboratory disappeared around me. Had it been destroyed? I couldn't tell. Everything around me had grown faint and hazy. I saw the sun hopping swiftly across the sky, leaping it every minute—every minute marking a day.

"On and on I traveled, still gaining speed. I saw huge buildings rise up, only to pass like dreams. The whole surface of the earth seemed to change, melting and flowing under my very eyes. My pace was now over a year a minute.

"Then, an uneasy feeling came over me. When should I stop? And if I did, would the machine and I occupy the same space as some other object? What would happen then? Would we be blown sky high in some sort of molecular explosion? As long as I kept this blinding speed, I knew I'd be safe. But I also knew I'd have to stop sometime.

"Finally, summoning my courage, I reached over and pushed the second lever forward. But I must have done it too quickly. For the machine spun hard onto its side, flinging me headlong through the air.

"A loud clap of thunder rang in my ears as I fell onto the soft, moist ground of a little lawn. I found myself in a heavy hailstorm. Seconds later, I was wet to the skin. Picking myself up, I looked around at this strange new land. A huge statue loomed over me in the haze of hail pelting down. It was made of white marble and shaped like a winged sphinx, with its wings spread out to the side. The base was made of bronze, turned green from the rain and sun and wind. And its sightless eyes seemed to be watching me.

"The hailstorm began to taper off as I turned to my time machine, now lying on its side. Heaving with all my strength, I managed to get it upright. This made me feel better, since escape through time now seemed possible again, if it were necessary.

"Then I looked at the machine's dial. It read 802,701 A.D. Was it possible? Had I traveled over eight thousand centuries into the future? The thought staggered me, even as the sky brightened with sunlight.

"Suddenly, the sound of approaching voices snapped me to attention. Coming through the bushes by the White Sphinx, as I named it, were the heads and shoulders of men running. One of them came straight up to me, laughing.

"He was about four feet in height and dressed in a purple tunic. He was young and graceful, handsome too, but somehow looked very frail. Some of the others now came closer. They spoke to each other in a strange, sweet language.

"Because they were so frail-looking, I felt confident I

could fight them off if they decided to attack me. But all they did was touch me—as if to prove I really existed. They were quite gentle, smiling and speaking to each other in a soft, cooing tone.

"I pointed to the machine and to myself, trying to make them understand what happened. But their faces were blank. They hadn't a clue.

"I pointed up toward the sun, hoping they'd understand the passing of days and nights. One of the young men made a booming noise with his mouth and cheeks. That's when I remembered the clap of thunder from before. I suddenly realized that they thought I had dropped from the sun in a thunderstorm!

"I could barely hide my disappointment. Had I come so far forward in time to be with people who had gone so far backward in intelligence? The question gnawed at me as one of the creatures placed a chain of beautiful flowers around my neck.

"The creatures led me past the White Sphinx toward a vast gray building of carved stone. At one time it must have been magnificent, but it had long since fallen into disrepair and was quite weather-worn. Inside was a huge hall, with tables made of polished stone slabs and laden with fruit. Around and between the tables were cushions for sitting. A few hundred people, as young and frail as those I first met, were eating the fruit. Some of it I recognized—raspberries and oranges—but much of it was strange to me. Hunger quickly got the better of me, and I eagerly joined the feast.

"Once fed, I did a bit of exploring outside the great hall. I found no evidence of any dogs, cattle, sheep, horses, weeds, or fungi. It seemed the whole earth had become a

16

garden. I saw brilliantly colored butterflies flitting about. There were no small houses. Instead, a few palace-like buildings could be seen among the greenery. I also saw what looked like some sort of wells, which seemed oddly out of place in this landscape.

"None of the young men and women I saw suffered from any obvious disease, nor did I see any of them doing any form of labor. Had they succeeded in creating a world free of pain, hunger, toil, old age, and fear?

"I concluded it must be so. The thought soothed me as I climbed a hill and watched the sun set over the lush countryside. What a marvelous land, I thought. Below lay the White Sphinx. And in front of it was the little lawn— but my time machine was nowhere to be seen!

Panic gripped me. I raced down the hill, falling once and cutting my chin. Over and over, I said to myself, 'They must have moved it a little, pushed it under the bushes out of the way.' But when I reached the lawn, my worst fears were realized. Not a trace of my machine did I find.

"The machine could not have moved through time; before I left it, I had taken its levers with me to prevent such an occurrence. And as weak and frail as they appeared, the little people would have had an impossible time removing it from the area. But what other answer was there? Could it be there was some other power at work that I had not suspected before?

"In a frenzy, I dashed about the bushes near the White Sphinx, searching for whatever signs I could find in the moonlight. As I did, I scared off some white animal, which I took to be a small deer.

"Sobbing and anguished, I went back to the great hall, now dark and silent except for the sound of people sleeping. I lit a match, then grabbed someone nearby. 'Where is my time machine? What have you done with it?' I screamed at him. His look, still sleepy, told me he had no idea what I was talking about.

"I knocked someone over as I bolted from the hall and out again into the moonlight. I went back to the lawn in front of the White Sphinx. Fatigue and grief swept over me. No sooner did I lie down than I was fast asleep on the soft grass.

"I awoke the next morning in sunlight. I wiped the sleep from my eyes and looked more closely at the ground. I saw a groove ripped in it, and odd, narrow footprints that could have been made by some sort of sloths. The groove disappeared underneath the bronze base of the White Sphinx. I now knew where my time machine was hidden—inside that base!

"I examined the panels of the base and saw that they were slightly uneven. That meant they might open somehow. I rapped against one panel and heard a hollow sound echoing from inside. I also thought I heard something stir inside— and what sounded like a laugh.

Over the next day or two, I managed to control my fear about losing my time machine forever. I went again with the young, slender creatures to the hall, and I explored the surrounding countryside some more. From atop other hills, I saw more of those peculiar wells, which seemed to be quite deep.

"I decided to look at one more closely. As I drew near it, I saw that its rim was made of bronze, much like the base of the White Sphinx, and was protected from the rain and hail by a kind of rough dome. Peering down the dark shaft, I saw no gleam of water, nor could I see anything reflecting from the bottom when I lit a match.

"But I did hear a thud-thud-thud, like the beating of some big engine. I also discovered, from the flaring of my match, that a strong, steady stream of air moved down the shaft. The only thing I could think of was that this was part of some large, underground fresh-air system. But fresh air for what? For whom?

"The next morning, I was still trying to figure this all out near a stream where some of the little people were playing. A weak cry came from up the stream. One of the young women was drifting out into the water. The current was swift, but not so swift that an average swimmer couldn't pull out of it. Yet the young woman floated on helplessly, and no one on the shore raised a finger to help her.

"I jumped in and waded after the poor thing. Once I caught her, I swam to shore. She was cold and shivering, and I rubbed her limbs to warm them. When she seemed all right, I left her. I thought that was that. But that afternoon, we met again. She greeted me with cries of delight

and gave me a big garland of flowers. I was touched by the gesture, and I tried to talk with her. In the past few days, I had managed to learn a few dozen words in their simple vocabulary. After a while, I found out her name: Weena.

"Like the other little people, Weena was fearless during the daylight. But at night, they were all deathly afraid of the dark, maybe even of their own shadows. They slept in droves inside the great halls and palaces. I never found one of them outside sleeping alone.

"That didn't stop me, however. I insisted on sleeping away from these slumbering masses. Weena, once she overcame her fear, sometimes slept not far from me.

"One very hot morning . . . it must have been my fourth in this strange land . . . I was seeking shelter from the heat and glare. For it was much hotter then than it is now. Perhaps the sun was hotter, or the earth closer to it.

"I found a colossal ruin close to the great hall where I fed. And clambering among the heaps of stone, I found a narrow passageway. As I came in from the dazzling sunlight, spots of color swam before my eyes. It was then that I noticed a pair of large, grayish-red eyes watching me out of the darkness.

"I reached for the creature, but it darted away. I could see well enough now to notice its dull, white color. Searching for it, I found instead another one of those well-like openings. Could the creature have disappeared down there? I looked down inside it, and sure enough, a pair of grayish-red eyes looked up at me. The creature was scampering down the side of the shaft, where metal foot- and hand-rests formed a kind of ladder.

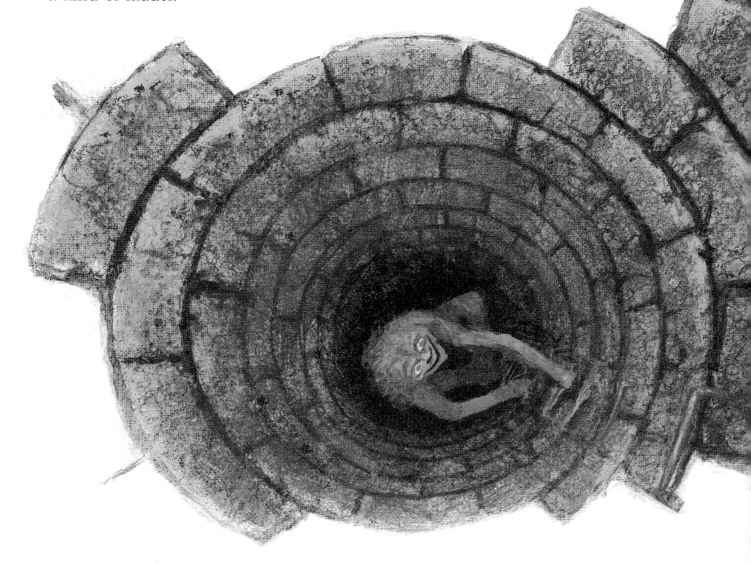

"It occurred to me that the earth beneath my feet had been tunneled to a large extent and that these creatures lived down in those tunnels. I asked the little people what these underground creatures were and did. But all I could learn was their name: Morlocks. I also finally learned the name of the race to which Weena and her companions belonged: Eloi.

"My mind went back to the small white animal I had startled in the bushes near the White Sphinx, searching for my time machine that first night. It had to have been a Morlock. But why had the Morlocks stolen my machine? And why wouldn't the Eloi help restore my machine to me?

"I pressed Weena on this point, but she burst into tears. They were the only tears, except my own, that I ever saw shed in that strange land I had stumbled into.

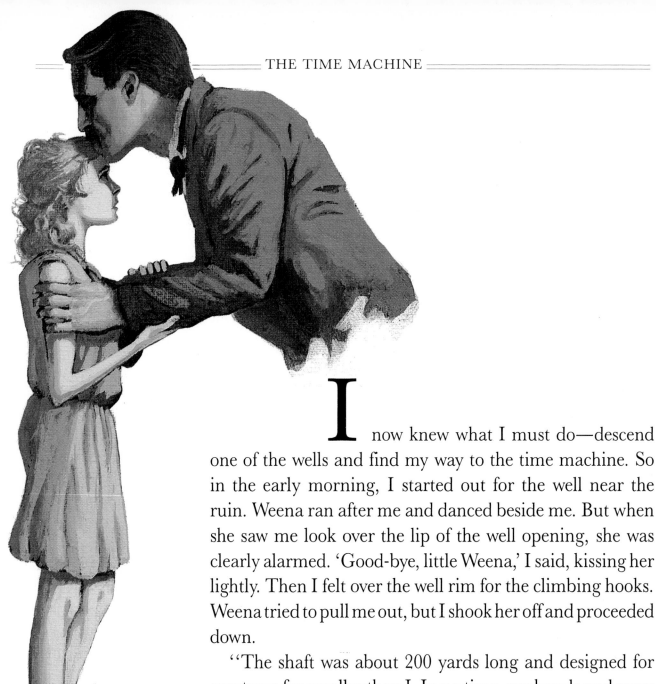

I now knew what I must do—descend one of the wells and find my way to the time machine. So in the early morning, I started out for the well near the ruin. Weena ran after me and danced beside me. But when she saw me look over the lip of the well opening, she was clearly alarmed. 'Good-bye, little Weena,' I said, kissing her lightly. Then I felt over the well rim for the climbing hooks. Weena tried to pull me out, but I shook her off and proceeded down.

"The shaft was about 200 yards long and designed for creatures far smaller than I. In no time, my hands and arms cramped and my back ached from the descent. I decided to rest for a few moments. Suddenly, one of the metal hooks I was holding bent off into the blackness below, leaving me dangling by one hand. Only luck saved me from certain death, and I did not dare rest again!

"The thudding sound of a machine grew louder and louder below as I continued downward. Then, just to the right of me, I discovered a slender loophole in the wall. Swinging myself into it, I found it was a small opening for a narrow horizontal tunnel. It was a place where I could lie down and rest.

"Still trembling from my near-fatal fall, I lay quietly—for how long, I cannot say. I was startled by a soft hand touching my face. Incredibly cold it was! I groped in the darkness for my matches and lit one. Three stooping white creatures, much like the one I had seen in the ruin, hastily retreated from the light.

"I was tempted to flee myself, to bolt out of the tunnel and up the ladder of metal hooks. But I was curious about the noise coming from farther down the tunnel. 'You are in for it now,' I whispered to myself, moving onward.

"The thudding became louder still, then the walls fell away from me. I struck another match, and in its glow I could see that I had entered a vast arched cavern. Off in the darkness, I could also see pairs of grayish-red eyes staring at me.

"The cavern had a stuffy, musty smell. In the distance was a little table of white metal, laid with what appeared to be a meal.

"I felt a hot stinging in my fingertips. The match had burned down, and I instinctively let it fall, a wriggling red spot in the blackness. As the darkness swept over me, I couldn't help thinking that I had come to this world poorly prepared. All I had to defend myself against the Morlocks were hands, feet, teeth . . . and four remaining matches!

"A hand touched mine. Then a set of icy-cold fingers crept over my face. An awful smell seemed no farther than a breath away from my nose now. And it chilled me to the bone to realize that it *was* a breath, *many* breaths, exhaled by a swarm of those dreadful little beings.

"They were pawing at me, plucking at my clothes, and making eerie laughing noises. I felt for another match and lit it, using a scrap of paper in my pocket to increase the flame. The Morlocks backed off, and I backed out of the cavern as fast as my feet would carry me.

"But as soon as I entered the tunnel, my flame blew out! In the darkness, I could hear the Morlocks rustling like wind among the leaves and pattering like the rain. They were racing toward me!

"I was seized by several pairs of hands, clawing and clutching. The Morlocks were trying to haul me back. I fumbled for another match and managed to strike it. The sudden flame drove them off again. Cupping the match to

protect it from any breath or gust of air, I backpedaled fast once more. When the second match burned down almost completely, I used it to light a third. By the time I reached the opening to the vertical shaft, this third match was just an ember.

"I gripped one of the metal hooks to start my climb upward. But before I could climb a single hook, my feet were grabbed from behind and pulled violently backward. I immediately lit my fourth and final match. But it went out! Kicking as hard as I could, I pulled free of their hands and sped up the shaft. Only one of the Morlocks continued the chase—and he almost claimed my shoe as a trophy.

"The last twenty or thirty feet to the top were the hardest. I felt lightheaded and totally exhausted as I struggled up and over the rim opening. The sunlight was blinding. And no sooner had I tumbled onto the soil, smelling sweet and clean in my nostrils, than I passed out.

When I awoke, I was surrounded by Weena and a few other Eloi. They seemed glad—relieved, really—to see me on the surface again. Unlike the Eloi, however, I was determined to defend myself from the Morlocks if they should attack me once more. I would find or make some sort of weapon to use against them. And I would find a safer place to sleep.

"Exploring toward the southwest, I saw in the distance a vast green structure. It was much larger than any of the other palaces or ruins I had seen. The face of it had a pale tint, like that seen on a kind of Chinese porcelain. And that's what I called it: the Palace of Green Porcelain.

"It was early evening when I started out for it and well past sunset when I was in easy sight of it. Weena came along with me. At times, she picked flowers and stuck them inside my pockets. I must admit, I was glad to have her company. There were moments when I felt very lonely, as if I were the only thinking human being left on earth.

"During our journey, the heel of one of my shoes became loose. A nail holding the sole together slowly worked its way up into the bottom of my foot, making me limp. Twilight deepened into night as we came to an open hill. Ahead lay a thick wood spreading wide and black before us, and past that lay the Palace of Green Porcelain, still far off. I decided to pass the night on top of the hill. Weena, tired from the travel, was soon fast asleep beside me. I took off my jacket and wrapped it around her. She slept peacefully as I sat and looked up at the stars twinkling in the clear night sky. I stayed that way all night long, watching for signs of any Morlocks. None came.

"When the sun rose in the east, I stood up and tested my legs. My foot had puffed out at the ankle and was painful under the heel. So I sat down again, took both shoes off, and flung them away. Then I awakened Weena, and the two of us headed into the wood to look for food.

"Gathering food was a new experience for Weena. Her days were spent not in labor, but in idle play. As we ate the ripe fruit we found dangling from trees and shrubs inside the wood, I pondered what to do next. My harrowing experience of the previous night seemed far away in the cheerful light of morning, but I was more determined than ever to confront the Morlocks again and defeat them once and for all. First, however, I had to get a weapon and find another source of fire now that my matches were gone. It was the one thing I knew the Morlocks were afraid of. I was equally determined to find some method—even a battering ram—to break open the White Sphinx's bronze panels that separated me from my time machine.

"Weena and I walked on until we reached the Palace of Green Porcelain. It was indeed made of porcelain, peeling and worn by the weather. The huge doors to the palace had been broken open. Inside was a long hallway sunlit by many side windows of jagged glass. The tiled floor was thick with gray dust, and I saw many different objects shrouded in the same dust.

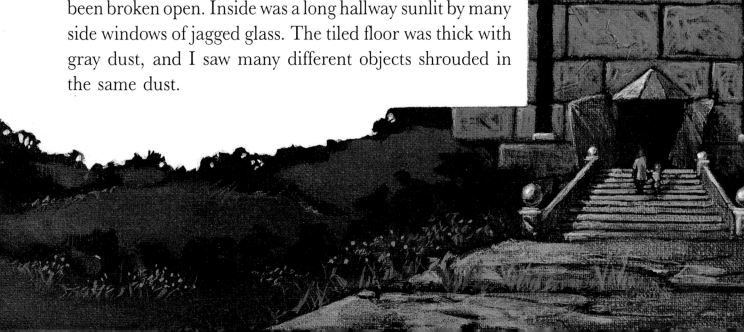

"In the center of the hallway stood the lower part of a large skeleton. The odd foot bones reminded me of a giant ground sloth's. They could have been those of a Megatherium, the largest known prehistoric ground sloth. Farther inside the hallway was the huge skeleton of what could only have been an Apatosaurus, a plant-eating dinosaur that lived over a hundred million years ago. A museum! It could be nothing else, I concluded. The fossils I saw proved it.

"Weena and I moved farther down the hall, which seemed to slope underneath our feet. I was excited by the possibility of finding a museum library here. Then I might be able to read about the world I now inhabited!

"As we walked on, I noticed the light growing fainter and fainter. We were moving slightly downward, and the outside ground was rising up on the windows, reducing the available sunlight. To our sides now were the corroded hulks of huge machines. And ahead lay darkness.

"The covering of dust on the floor before us was broken up by small narrow footprints. And I could now hear the same odd noises I had heard down the shaft of the well. Weena squeezed my hand in fear. We both knew the Morlocks were nearby. That's when I reached over to a machine and yanked off an iron lever sticking out from it. This mace would come in handy for any future encounters with the Morlocks.

"With the iron mace in one hand and Weena holding my other, I left that hallway and entered an even larger one. Tattered flags hung from the walls. But on closer inspection, I realized these flags were the decaying remains of books! This library was now a wilderness of rotting paper—the printed words having long since faded away.

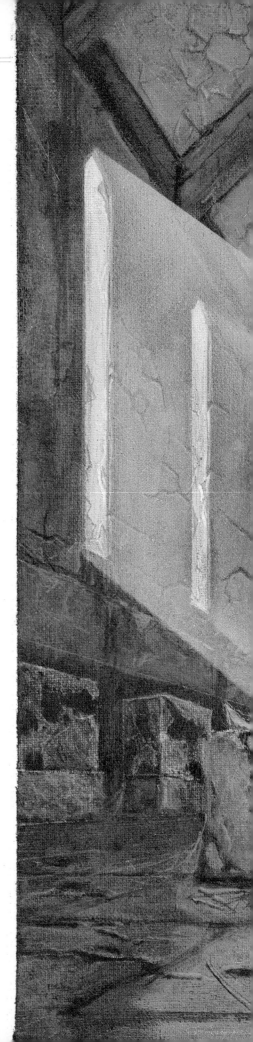

"Deeply disappointed, I moved on with Weena at my side. A broad staircase led us up to a hall filled with various chemicals and tubes and glass cases. The cases seemed to be airtight, and to my delight I found a box of matches in one. I removed a match and struck it against the coarse side of the box. It burst into flame. The matches were still good! And my luck held when I found a sealed jar of camphor crystals, which I knew burned with a bright flame.

"For the rest of the day, until dusk, we explored the other great halls inside the Palace of Green Porcelain. We came across galleries of rusting pistols, rifles, and swords, as well as exotic objects collected from what seemed like every corner of the world.

"I left the palace feeling hopeful. I had a weapon and a source of fire. Now all I had to do was find a safe, open spot where Weena and I could keep a fire going as we slept. Then, the next morning, I'd go straight to the White Sphinx and try to break down its doors. Escaping this dreaded time and place on earth was uppermost in my thoughts—and I intended to bring Weena with me.

We traveled as far as we could toward the White Sphinx. Along the way, I collected sticks and dried grass for the fire I intended to build that night. But the load of wood and grass slowed me down, and Weena grew tired from all the walking we had done. I was tired myself, having gone without sleep for a night and two days. Darkness was rapidly closing in on us, making me drowsier.

"Then, from the black bushes behind us, I heard a twig snap. I turned and saw three crouching creatures. I hurried ahead, and I could hear Weena panting from our faster pace. I felt if we could get free of the wood and onto the bare side of a hill just beyond it, we'd be all right.

''Finally, I decided to put down the firewood and grass I was carrying to lighten my load and quicken our escape. Then I realized if I were to light this fire, it would likely scare off the Morlocks behind us. I took out a match and lit the pile. Red tongues of flame went licking up the wood. Weena was fascinated by this burning heap and would have tried to play with it had I not stopped her.

''We plunged ahead, the fire's light dimming with each step we took. Soon we were in total darkness once more. Weena clutched my hand in fright. I slipped my arm around her and carried her now. My right hand was still holding the iron lever.

"The sound of my own heavy breathing filled my ears. Then I heard something else—a pattering of feet, followed by odd voices. The Morlocks were getting closer!

"Suddenly, I felt a tug on my coat, then something at my arm. I was frantic to light a match. But to do that, I had to put Weena down. Reluctantly, I eased her onto the ground and searched for a match in my pocket. A struggle began in the darkness around my knees. The Morlocks were trying to take Weena! Cold hands slithered along my body, too, even reaching my neck. That's when I found a match and scratched it on the side of the box. It fizzed into flame, driving off the Morlocks.

"Weena lay motionless at my feet. Had they killed her?

I stooped down beside her. She was still breathing, though she was unconscious.

"I picked Weena up and carefully placed her over my shoulder. Then I pushed on. But I stopped after a few steps. In the confusion of the Morlock attack, I had turned myself around a few times. Now I didn't know which direction to take. *Think!* I said to myself. *THINK!*

"But it was no use. I couldn't figure out the correct path forward. I gently put Weena back down and lit a piece of camphor. Then I gathered some sticks and leaves to fan its flame. From the corners of my eyes, I could see the grayish-red gaze of the Morlocks watching me. They were waiting for the fire to die out.

"To my horror that's exactly what happened! A second before I could put the twigs and leaves on the flame, it went out. I lit another match, and two white forms approaching Weena dashed hastily away. Another was so blinded by the sudden light that it rushed straight at me! I swung my fist, knocking it back. I wasted no time in gathering more wood and leaves for the fire. Soon, I had a smoky, choking fire blazing.

"The rhythmic crackling of the burning twigs and the smell of camphor in the night's air made my eyelids heavy. I seemed to nod off for a moment, then open my eyes. But all was dark around me. Instantly, I realized that I had just awakened from a deep sleep. And now the fire was out!

"Then the Morlocks attacked me. Prying their fingers off me as best I could, I felt in my pocket for my box of matches. It was gone! The Morlocks' hands gripped me again—tighter this time, almost choking me. I was caught

by the neck, head, and arms. I felt teeth nipping at me, and rolled over in a panic. As I did, my hand brushed against the iron lever.

"Grabbing it firmly, I rose up and swung the bar in a small, powerful arc. I could feel it smash into the cold hands, arms, and bodies of the Morlocks. I backed up against a tree, still swinging wildly. With my last breath, I would lash back at them, taking as many with me as I could.

"Then something extraordinary happened. The Morlocks backed away. In fact, they were running from me. Why? Had I really beaten them back?

"The answer came a moment later. The darkness surrounding me had grown oddly bright. Then I saw a red spark drift across the gap between two overhanging branches. A whiff of smoking wood reached my nose. Stepping around the tree at my back, I saw a tremendous fire burning toward me. It was my first fire come after me. And worse still, little Weena had disappeared!

With huge trees bursting into flame behind me, I had no time to think—just flee. Clutching my iron bar, I followed in the Morlocks' path. The race between the fire and myself was close, but at last I emerged in a small open space. *Safe,* I thought, *for the moment.*

"I was wrong. A Morlock, panicked by the blaze, blundered toward me. I sidestepped him and, blinded as he was by the light, he went straight into the fire! Then I saw a whole band of Morlocks—thirty or forty of them— on a hill at the center of the open space where I stood. They were running amok, some bowling each other over, others heading right for me. I fended them off with my bar. But then I realized they were far more afraid of the fire than of my iron mace, and I merely dodged them after that.

''Three times I saw a few Morlocks lower their heads and try to run through the flames now encircling us. None made it. Their cries rang through the night as the fire raged on. By the time dawn came, the fire had dwindled down to glowing embers. All that could be seen were charred trees, scorched earth, and streaming masses of black smoke floating up into the air. Only a few Morlocks remained, dazed and drained of energy by the night's fire. They posed no threat to me.

''I searched and searched for Weena, but I could find no trace of her. Filled with sadness, I headed for the White Sphinx with my mace. In the bright sunshine of morning, it felt like the darkest day for me yet in this miserable world. Never before had I felt so lonely. My only consolation was that in placing my hand into my trouser pocket, I found some loose matches. They must have fallen out of the box before it was lost.

With a full day of sunlight ahead of me, I decided to lie down and rest awhile on a soft patch of grass not far from the White Sphinx. When I awoke, just before sunset, I felt strong and confident. I made a beeline for the White Sphinx. I was determined to smash in the bronze panels with the iron bar I held in my hands.

"But when I got there, I was stunned. The panels were open! They had slid down into grooves in the ground. And inside, sitting in a corner, was my time machine.

"I could still feel in my pocket the two levers I had unscrewed from the machine. Tossing aside the iron mace, I walked toward the machine. With a thunderous clang, the bronze panels shut behind me—as I had expected. I was thrust into darkness. Trapped. Or so the Morlocks thought.

"You see, I still had the loose matches in my pocket. Very calmly, I tried to light one. But I had overlooked one thing—these were matches that could only be lit on the box.

"When I realized that, fear froze me to the spot. Then I made a mad scramble for the seat of the machine. The Morlocks lunged at me in the darkness. Hands clutched at me from everywhere, and I could hear teeth gnashing close to my ears. I hit one Morlock after another with the levers I had removed from my pocket. I succeeded in screwing one lever in. But a Morlock grabbed hold of the other, nearly prying it loose from me. I butted my head against his, knocking him back. Then I quickly screwed in the second lever and pushed it forward.

"The clinging hands of the Morlocks slipped away. I was once more hurtling through time. My nightmare, I thought, was finally over."

Epilogue

I glanced at my fellow dinner guests. None of us knew what to say. We had listened to our host's story for nearly an hour without interruption, as he had requested. It was amazing, fantastic, and—

"Unbelievable, gentlemen?" our host suddenly asked. "Do you think I dreamed all this in my workshop?"

The newspaper editor spoke now. "What a pity you're not a writer of stories." He went over and placed a hand on our host's shoulder.

"You don't believe it?"

"Well . . ."

"I thought not."

Then our host reached into his pocket and pulled out two withered white flowers. The doctor examined them closely. "Hmmm," he said, almost to himself, "I've never seen these anywhere before. Where did you get them?"

"From Weena," said our host. I could see the frustration in his face now. "Come, gentlemen."

With that, he picked up a lamp and walked swiftly toward his laboratory. We followed him. Opening the door, he shone the light inside. "See for youselves!" There, in the flickering lamplight, was the time machine—smeared with grass and dotted with bits of moss, with one rail bent.

"It's moved," I remarked, almost to myself.

"Yes," said our host. "It's moved precisely the distance between where my machine landed on the grass in front of the White Sphinx and where the Morlocks dragged it inside the bronze panels."

We all left soon after. I could tell none of the others believed him. But after a sleepless night spent thinking about it, I decided to visit him alone the next day.

When I arrived, he seemed very busy. He carried a small camera in one hand, and had a knapsack under his other arm. "Please sit down for a while," he said, "and I'll be with you shortly."

I did as I was told. But I suddenly remembered another appointment I had to keep that day. I started to look for

our host to tell him. Not finding him in the house, I went to the laboratory. As I reached for the doorknob, I heard a slight cry, then a click, then a thud.

I opened the door immediately. A gust of air whirled around me. Glass shattered and fell from the laboratory windows. And before me was a ghostly, spinning outline of the time machine with my host sitting inside it. Then, both man and machine vanished.

Where did he go? Did he return to Weena? Had he gone back into the past this time? I don't know. No one knows. And except for myself, no one believes any of it. All I know for certain is that he disappeared three years ago—and has never returned.

But I have as a reminder Weena's strange white flowers, shriveled now, and brown and flat and brittle. Somehow they are proof to me that even when mind and strength are gone, gratitude and mutual tenderness can still live on in the human heart.